Certificate

This is to certify that

....

has received his/her

diploma from the Sarah Webb

'Kids Can Cook'

School of Cookery

having mastered all the

recipes in this book

ZOË
"WE MADE CHOCOLATE BISCUIT CAKE AND IT WAS FUN. I ATE IT ALL UP – ALL OF IT!" (PAGE 63.)
SAM
"MUM, LET'S MAKE MORE OF THAT YUMMY, YUMMY CAKE" (MOTHER'S DAY CAKE, PAGE 70.)
EMMA
"THE MOORE STREET BANANAS WERE A BIG SUCCESS. THE KIDS LOVED MAKING THEM – AND I LOVED EATING THEM!" (PAGE 36.)
SINÉAD
"I THOUGHT SCONES WOULD BE DIFFICULT BUT THEY WERE REALLY EASY. MY FRIENDS THINK THEY'RE BRILL AND ASK FOR MORE – WITH JAM AND CREAM." (PAGE 86.)

Sarah Webb

KIDS CAN COOK

Illustrated by Terry Myler

THE CHILDREN'S PRESS

TO

Andrew, Niamh, Neil, Sam, Sarah, Siobhra, Tanya and my family, all the gang at Waterstone's, Children's Books Ireland, Children's Press, and the wonderful nurses and doctors at the National Children's Hospital (Harcourt Street).

First published 1997 by
The Children's Press
an imprint of Anvil Books
45 Palmerston Road, Dublin 6

ISBN 1 901737 03 9

Typeset by Computertype Limited
Printed by Colour Books Limited
Back cover photograph: Siobhra Hooper

Contents

Introduction

My first memory of cooking was making little men out of left-over pastry scraps. Mum would pop these into the oven with the pie she was baking. My little creations would come out hot and golden brown and I ate them then and there.

My family and I spent every summer in Castletownshend in West Cork. We had no television in the house we rented there, and when my sisters, Kate and Emma, and I were young we found lots of ways to amuse ourselves – reading, boating and swimming, playing games and cooking. My dad would take us grocery shopping to Field's in Skibbereen, where we would buy delicious crusty bread, cheese and fresh vegetables. Then my sisters and I would cook the evening meal and fight over who was to do the washing up!

Now I have a son of my own, Sam, and we enjoy cooking together.

Cooking is fun, and with the help of this book you can create tasty food for your family and friends. Many are traditional Irish recipes, such as Donegal Potato Cakes and Barm Brac. All are easy to make and great to eat. You can find out how pot-ovens and griddles were used to cook in olden times in 'A Little History'. And finally some well-known authors share their favourite recipes with you.

So get out those wooden spoons, put on your aprons and get cooking!

Before you start have a look at the next few pages to pick up safety tips and hints on cookery terms you may not recognize.

A special word of thanks to my loyal gang of young chefs who tested the recipes: Sinead, Sean and Barbara, Emma and Zoe, Gillian, Clarice and Brian, and Sam.

A Little History

Ireland in ancient days was covered in woods of pine, hazel, birch and oak. The earliest Irish people were hunter-gatherers they hunted animals and ate their meat, and collected wild berries and fruit from the land to eat. Coastal settlers ate sea food, fish and shellfish such as mussels. Today there are special places called 'shell middens' where the discarded remains of shells can be seen.

Gradually life began to change and Irish people started to cut down the trees and farm the land. This happened between 4000 and 3000 BC and changed the way of life and way of eating. Pigs were kept for their meat and cattle for their meat and milk. Cereals such as oats and wheat, coarsely ground using millstones, were grown and porridge and bread could be made. These early breads may even have damaged teeth, as archaeologists have found medieval skeletons with worn-down teeth!

When Ireland was Christianized (about the late fourth and early fifth centuries) the monks and holy men who recorded the events of the time in manuscripts, included details of foods and eating habits. The main foods were milk and dairy products, eggs, cereals, meats, rabbit, game, vegetables, fish, fruit and honey. Milk was a favourite drink, drunk either fresh or sour; ingredients such as rennet or butterwort could be used to sour it. Butter was very important as the bread was coarse and dry, and sometimes herbs or salt were added to give it a more appetising taste.

Other important foods were cheese made with cow or goat, sometimes even sheep, milk. Eggs were eaten. Hen and goose eggs came from the farms and sea-bird eggs were collected in coastal areas. The Irish were not great vegetable eaters at that time. Cabbage and some types of early turnip were grown, and apples and wild berries were known from very early days. Honey was a popular sweetener as there was no sugar (honeyed salmon was said to be delicious).

Between the twelfth and seventeenth centuries Ireland was invaded and colonised by many different armies, each bringing their own customs and their own foods. But the most important development in the history of food in Ireland was the introduction, in the 1700s, of the potato. Visitors to Ireland noted that 'a very limited portion of land, a few days labour and a small amount of manure, will create a stock upon which a family

may exist for twelve months'. It was also noted that 'almost every soil will produce potatoes'.

It was because of the potato that the population of Ireland grew so dramatically between the eighteenth and nineteenth centuries to over eight million. And over a third of this population subsisted almost entirely on the potato crop, sometimes, but not always, supplemented by buttermilk.

The menu of the poor was enshrined in the verse:

Pratai i maidin,
Pratai san lo,
Agus ma eirighim san oiche,
Praitai a geobhainn.

('Potatoes in the morning, potatoes in the day, and if I got up at night, potatoes I would get.')

But the potato was subject to a terrible disease – potato blight – in which the potatoes turned black, rotted and became inedible. There were several partial famines in Ireland, the most catastrophic of which was the Great Famine of 1846. Between the years 1845 to 1850, Ireland lost over three million people due to death and emigration.

Though potatoes are no longer the staple item of diet for us in Ireland, we are still the biggest eaters of potatoes in Europe, reflected in the many recipes based on the potato which you will find in every cookery book.

After the Famine, Irish people turned more to bread as an essential food. Most of the people had no ovens and cooked in the pot-oven, a heavy, black, shallow pot with a lid which was placed on the open fire and covered in hot coals or burning turf. The griddle was a round iron plate which had two handles or 'ears'. It rested on a small three-legged stand over the fire and was used to griddle bread or potato cakes.

This century has seen a complete change in eating habits. Now we import foods from all over the world – curry from India, pasta from Italy, and exotic fruits such as passion fruit and kiwis. Food has become more interesting and exciting, and menus in hotels and restaurants reflect this.

So when you start cooking, think how lucky you are! In the olden days, you would have had to cook on a complicated oven with no set temperatures. You would also have had to rely on fresh ingredients for most recipes as there were no fridges or freezers then (food was placed in a wooden box, with a door and sides of fine mesh to keep out insects and allow air to circulate, placed in a cool, draughty corridor).

Cookery Words

In cooking, special tools or utensils are needed for different jobs, such as peelers and electric blenders. Special terms such as kneading and grating are used to describe cookery skills.

Here are some of the most commonly used words you will come across in these recipes:

Beating means mixing ingredients (such as butter) together to form a smooth paste, using a wooden spoon (and elbow power). If you soften the butter first in the oven or microwave, this makes it easier to work with. But be careful; a second or two will do.

Blending also means mixing together, this time with an electric blender. It is the easiest way to combine solid and liquid ingredients (such as bananas and milk – for a milkshake). Use the blender with great care and keep fingers well away. Better still, ask an adult for help.

Creaming. Butter and sugar sometimes need to be 'creamed'. Cut the butter into small pieces and add to the sugar. Mix together with a wooden spoon until light and creamy.

Cutting. Use a sharp knife – *! watch fingers* – and always cut on a chopping board to prevent marking a counter or table-top.

Dicing means cutting into small pieces or cubes.

Folding in. When a recipe tells you to 'fold' one ingredient into another, this means mixing with great care. Beaten egg whites and flour are one example. Take a metal spoon and gently turn the mixture over and over in the bowl. If you 'fold in' carelessly or too quickly the beaten-up egg whites will collapse and you won't get the lightness the recipe demands.

Grating. Ingredients often need to be 'grated' into small fragments. The usual household grater has two to four sides, each giving a different kind of shred, from fine to coarse.

Kneading. When making bread or pastry the dough may need to be 'kneaded' or worked together with your hands. Put the dough on a floured table-top or counter, making sure it's steady. Using your two hands, stretch the dough, then pull it together. Give the dough a quarter turn and repeat, again and again. Keep doing this until the dough is smooth and stretchy.

Mashing. Vegetables such as potatoes and parsnips often need to be 'mashed', or squashed, into a smooth mixture. This is done with a masher. If you haven't got one, use a fork.

Oven thermometer. If your cooker doesn't have one built in, get a little free-standing one.

Peeling. Some fruit and vegetables may need to be 'peeled'. For this you need a special peeler. Hold the fruit or vegetable firmly in one hand and the peeler in the other and peel firmly towards yourself.

To 'peel' a tomato, drop it into boiling water for 1-2 minutes: the skin will slip off easily.

Rubbing in. To mix flour and butter together into small breadcrumb-sized pieces, rub them between your finger tips to form crumbs.

Seasoning. To 'season' means to flavour with salt and pepper or other herbs and spices. A 'pinch' means just that, a little piece pinched between your finger-tips and scattered over the ingredients.

Scraping. Vegetables with fine skins like new potatoes or parsnips can be peeled more easily if you use a 'scraper' rather than a peeler. Hold the scraper firmly and scrape away from yourself in short firm strokes.

Separating eggs. If you need to separate the egg white from the yellow yoke, break the egg on to a saucer. Place a cup over the yoke, tilt the saucer and catch the egg white in a bowl, leaving the yoke in the cup. Magic!

Shredding means cutting into thin ribbons (usually used for lettuce).

Simmering is a gentle boil. Make sure the liquid does not dry up or overflow and spill out of the pan. Always watch a saucepan simmering on a ring – just in case.

Slicing means cutting into thin slices.

Whisking. Some ingredients such as eggs and cream need to be 'whisked' to put air into them. You can use a manual or an electric whisk. The manual whisk has a handle which is turned quickly. As you use both hands (one to hold the whisk and one to turn the handle), you must make sure the bowl is steady. An easy way to stop it slipping is to rest it on a tea-towel.

If you have an electric whisk in the house, ask an adult for help to use it.

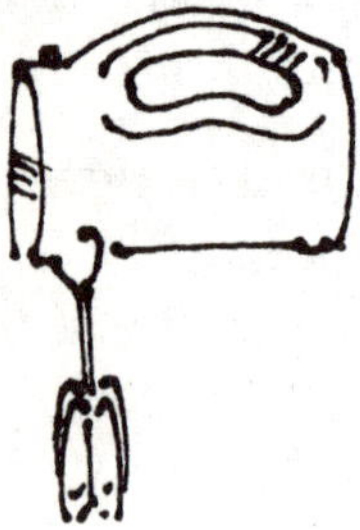

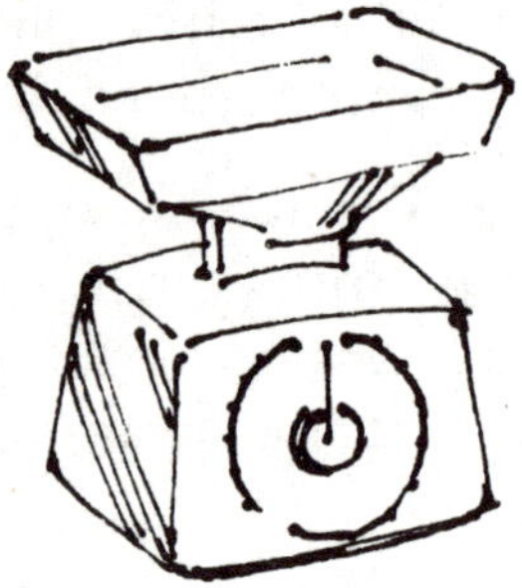

Weighing and measuring. A recipe may not work if you do not measure the ingredients correctly. Use a weighing scales to weigh flour and other dry ingredients and a measuring jug to measure liquids.

When measuring with a spoon, such as a teaspoon of sugar, the spoon should be level, not heaped.

WARNING! You can't be careful enough when using sharp knives, blenders, scrapers and peelers. Watch those fingers at all times, and, if you use electrical equipment, always have an adult at hand.

Safety First

Safety is important in the kitchen where you will be working with a lot of dangerous kitchen utensils such as knives, and kitchen machines such as blenders.

Top Nine Safety Tips

1) Make sure an **adult** is standing by, just in case. If there is anything you don't understand ask for help.
2) Watch your fingers with sharp **knives** and graters. The edges of cans are often sharp, so dispose of these very carefully.
3) Take great care with electrical **kitchen machines**. Make sure your hands are dry when plugging them in and out or you may get an electrical shock. Never open a blender when it is in use; this is dangerous; and also very messy as the ingredients will splatter out all over the walls and all over you.
4) Never leave the kitchen when the gas or electric rings are on. Always **turn off the rings, switches, knobs or gas** after you have finished cooking. Kitchens can be fire hazards, so be very careful.
5) Have a cloth or kitchen roll to hand in case of spills. Be especially careful to **mop up spills** on the floor, as you or someone else might slip.

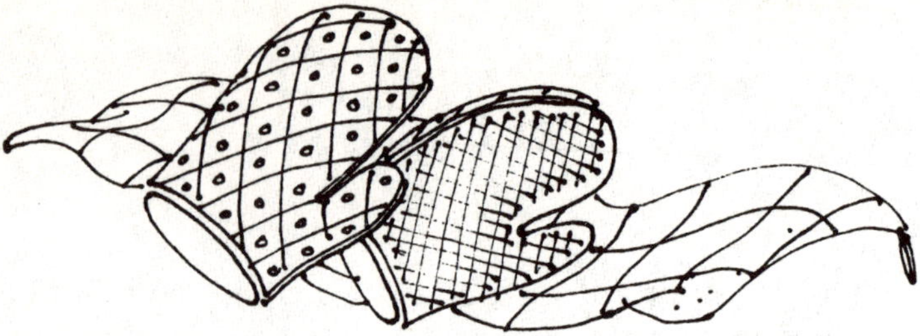

6) Always use **oven gloves** or a thick tea-towel when lifting hot dishes out of the oven. Use a heatproof mat or a chopping board to put hot dishes on – these can burn table or counter-tops.
7) Turn all **saucepan handles** to the side to avoid knocking them over by accident.
8) After cutting **raw meat, chicken or fish**, wash your hands, the knife and the chopping board carefully, as these raw ingredients can contain germs. Always store meat, chicken or fish in a secure container, away from other ingredients.
9) Ban all **pets** from the kitchen while you are cooking. They can carry germs and can also get under your feet and cause accidents.

   Sorry, Tiddles.

To recap:

1) Have an adult on stand-by.
2) Be careful with knives.
3) Be careful with electrical machines.
4) Turn off rings.
5) Wipe up spills.
6) Use oven gloves.
7) Saucepan handles in.
8) Wash after raw meat.
9) No pets.

First Aid

If you have an accident, call an adult at once. Even small cuts and burns may need a plaster. If the cut or burn is bad, get a doctor or nurse as soon as possible.

Burns: Place the burn under cold water for five minutes and cover with a clean bandage or plaster.

Cuts: Clean the cut under the tap and cover with a plaster.

Before You Start

1) Put on an apron, roll back your sleeves and tie back long hair.

2) Wash your hands.

3) Make sure the worktops and tabletops are clean.

4) Collect together all the ingredients and cooking utensils you will need for the recipe.

5) Read through the recipe and make sure you understand it. Ask for help if you need anything explained.

WHEN YOU SEE THE (!) SIGN BE EXTRA CAREFUL

Hot Stuff

Sam's Crispy Chicken

(serves 4)

An old Irish folk tale called 'The Cock' relates that when Jesus was buried they put a cock into a pot to boil. It was believed that when the cock rose up out of the pot and crowed twelve times, then the son of God had risen. And sure enough the cock crowed and Jesus rose from the dead.

Chicken is full of protein, especially when it's very fresh, so it's ideal for growing family members. My son Sam loves the crunchy fun topping of this recipe, so I named it after him.

4oz/100g butter
4 chicken fillets
6 bags cheese and onion crisps
2oz/50g grated cheese

Utensils: saucepan, wooden spoon, oven-proof dish, grater

Preheat the oven to gas mark 6 / 400 F° / 200 C°

---

1 Melt the butter in a saucepan.

2 Crush the crisps. The easiest way to do this is to squash them in the bag with your hands until they crumble into little pieces. Be very careful that the bags don't burst! Add the crisps to the butter and stir gently.

3 Place the chicken pieces in the oven-proof dish. Spoon the crisp mixture over the top.

4 Grate the cheese and sprinkle it over the crispy topping. Bake in the oven for 40-45 minutes.

5 Serve with potatoes and vegetables or a green salad and crunchy bread.

Yum!

Salmon Pie

(serves 4-6)

There are many Irish legends involving the salmon. The most famous is about Fionn MacCumhaill ('Finn McCool') and the Salmon of Knowledge. Fionn was cooking a magical salmon for his master Finneigeas over an open fire. While cooking it, he burnt his thumb and put it in his mouth to soothe the pain. This gave him the first taste of the Salmon of Knowledge and made him the wisest of men.

Another tale, *Children of the Salmon*, tells how a Queen of Ireland and her cook, who were unable to have children, ate an enchanted salmon and had identical sons. These boys grew up brave and strong, and they overcame a giant and witch before winning the hands of two beautiful princesses.

My recipe uses tinned salmon as fresh salmon is not always available.

---

1 large tin of salmon
1 cup breadcrumbs
4 oz/100g butter
1 large onion
2 eggs
a handful of fresh chopped parsley
salt and pepper

Utensils: mixing bowl, fork, cup, saucepan, wooden spoon, sharp knife, chopping board, small bowl, oven-proof dish

---

Preheat the oven to gas mark 5 / 190 C° / 373 C°

1 Place the salmon in the mixing bowl and mash, using a fork. Add half the breadcrumbs.

2 Melt the butter in a saucepan and add to the salmon mixture – *! watch the hot butter.*

3 Remove the outer skin of the onion and chop it into small pieces – *! watch fingers.*

4 Beat the eggs in a small bowl with a fork.

5 Add the parsley, onion, beaten egg and a pinch of salt and pepper to the salmon. Mix well with a wooden spoon.

6 Pour the mixture into a greased oven-proof dish and sprinkle the rest of the breadcrumbs over the top.

7 Bake for 25-30 minutes until golden brown.

8 Serve hot with potatoes and vegetables or cold with crunchy bread and green salad.

Irish Cheddar and Potato Bake

(serves 4-6)

Cheese was known in Ireland in pre-Christian times. It was made from goat and sheep's milk, as well as from cow's milk.

Cheese has its place in legend too. In the *Tain Bo Cuailige*, one of the great heroic sagas of Ireland, Queen Maeve is killed when her nephew Furbaidhe throws a piece of cheese at her forehead.

Ireland is famous throughout the world for

its cheeses, including Cashel Blue from Cashel and Gubbeen from Cork. My recipe combines Irish cheddar with potatoes.

---

6 large potatoes
1 large onion
1oz/25g butter
4oz/100g grated cheddar cheese (red or white)
salt and pepper
1 egg
$^{1}/_{2}$ pint/150ml single cream

Utensils: potato peeler, large bowl, sharp knife, chopping board, large saucepan, grater, oven-proof dish, fork, small bowl

---

Preheat the oven to gas mark 4 / 350 F° / 175 C°

---

1 Peel the potatoes and slice into thin pieces – *! watch fingers*. Place the pieces in a bowl of water.

2 Slice the onion into thin pieces – *! fingers*. Melt the butter in a saucepan and cook the onion over a low heat until slightly soft (5 – 6 minutes).

3 Grate the cheese – *! fingers*.

4 Grease an oven-proof dish.

5 Place a layer of potatoes on the bottom of the dish.

6 Add a layer of onions. Season with salt and pepper and sprinkle cheese on top.

7 Keep adding layers of potatoes, onions and cheese, finishing with a layer of potatoes.

8 Beat the egg into the cream with a fork. Pour the mixture over the potatoes and sprinkle the remaining cheese over the top.

9 Bake for 90 minutes.

Spring Onion and Cheese Omelette

(serves 2)

Eggs have always been a popular food and ingredient in Ireland. There is a mention of hens in the eighth-century Brehon Laws, and for hundreds of years eggs were bartered or swopped with shopkeepers for luxuries such as sugar and tea. In an old Irish tale, *The Widow's Son and the Wizard,* a young boy called Manus overcome a terrible wizard by throwing an egg at his forehead!

---

2 eggs
salt and pepper
2 oz/50g grated cheese
3 spring onions
knob of butter

Utensils: small bowl, fork, grater, sharp knife, chopping board, frying-pan

---

1 Break the eggs into a bowl. Add salt and pepper and beat lightly with a fork.

2 Grate the cheese – *! watch fingers.*

3 Chop the white ends of the spring onions into thin pieces.

4 Melt the butter in a frying-pan and swirl it around. When the butter foams, pour in the egg mixture.

5 When the omelette begins to set at the edges, sprinkle the cheese and spring onions over the top.

6 When the top has set, but is still creamy, fold the edges over and slip the omelette on to a plate.

7 Serve at once.

Simple Sausage Rolls

(makes 24)

One of the first recipes I learned to cook was sausage rolls. My Mum would help me to roll out and cut the pastry and I would prick the sausages and wrap them in little 'pastry overcoats' all by myself.

Sausages were made in ancient times. The word comes from the Latin salsus, meaning salted. The early sausages were dried or cured to preserve the meat and they were full of spices, rather like modern day Italian sausages.

Sausages rolls are easy to make and are great finger foods at a party.

---

1 packet frozen puff pastry (12oz/340g)
24 sausages
1 egg

Utensils: rolling-pin, sharp knife, small bowl, fork, pastry brush, baking tray

Preheat the oven to gas mark 6 / 400 F° / 200 C°

1 Allow the frozen pastry to thaw (defreeze) for $1^1/_2$ hours at room temperature.

2 Roll out the pastry on to a floured table-top or counter, using a lightly floured rolling-pin (the pastry should be about the thickness of a penny).

3 Cut the pastry into strips 6 inches wide using a sharp knife – *! watch fingers.*

4 Place a line of sausages on the centre of each strip.

5 Beat the egg with a fork in a small bowl.

6 Brush each side of the pastry with egg, using the pastry brush, and fold over the sausages.

7 Press the pastry edges together firmly.

8 Cut the pastry rolls into single sausage rolls with a sharp knife – *! fingers.*

9 Brush each roll with a little egg to give it a nice glaze (shine).

10 Place on a floured baking tray and bake for 30 minutes until golden brown.

Try making party bites by using cocktail sausages instead of the larger sausages.

Parsnip and Carrot Bake

(serves 4)

Carrots and parsnips are root vegetables; they grow underground. The goodness or nutrients are just under the skin, which is why they are scraped and not peeled. Carrots have a natural ingredient called orange carotenoid, which gives them their vivid colour. Carrots are also rich in vitamin A, important for sight and healthy growth of skin and tissues.

Some people are 'vegetarian', which means they eat no meat. This is a useful vegetarian main course to serve them.

---

1 lb/500g carrots
1 lb/500g parsnips
4oz/100g butter
salt and pepper
2oz/50g grated cheese (vegetarian cheese can be used)

Utensils: sharp knife or scraper, chopping board, saucepan, masher, oven-proof serving dish, grater

1 Scrape the carrots and parsnips with a sharp knife or scraper and slice into thin pieces – *! watch fingers.*

2 Place the vegetables in a saucepan and add cold water until they are just about covered.

3 Add half the butter to the water and bring to the boil. Simmer for 10-15 minutes until the vegetables are tender.

4 Add the rest of the butter and a pinch of salt and pepper. Mash the vegetables with the masher.

5 Place the vegetables in a warm serving dish. Sprinkle the top with grated cheese and grill for 2-3 minutes until the cheese has melted.

6 Serve piping hot.

Baltimore Fish Dish

(serves 4-6)

Every July my family and I pack up all our holiday gear – clothes, books, buckets, spades and life-jackets – and travel to Castletownshend in West Cork, where we spend our summer holidays. We take turns cooking and often on a day trip to Schull or Baltimore, pick up fresh fish from the local fishing boats.

This is a recipe which I cook for my family:

3 large potatoes
sprig of parsley
2oz/50g plain white flour
$^3/_4$ pint/425ml milk
salt and pepper
2oz/50g butter
2 lb/900g fillets of plaice or sole
6oz/175g grated cheese

Utensils: potato peeler, sharp knife, saucepan, chopping board, mixing bowl, measuring jug, wooden spoon, oven-proof dish, potato masher, metal spoon, grater

Preheat the oven to gas mark 6 / 400 F° / 200 C°

1 Peel the potatoes, cut into thick slices, and put them in a saucepan of water to boil for 15 – 20 minutes.

2 Cut the parsley into small pieces with a sharp knife – *! watch fingers*.

3 Place the flour in a mixing bowl and add the milk, parsley and a pinch of salt and pepper. Mix well with a wooden spoon.

4 Place the fillets in an oven-proof dish and pour the milk mixture over them.

5 Drain the water from the potatoes – *! watch hot water and steam*. Add the butter and a pinch of salt and pepper. Mash, using a potato masher.

6 Spoon the potato over the fish and milk mixture and sprinkle with grated cheese.

7 Cook for 30 minutes until the top is golden and crispy.

8 Serve hot with vegetables.

Irish Stew

(serves 4-6)

In past times, when potatoes were the main food, they were usually boiled in a large iron cauldron over the fire. To add flavour, meat such as lamb was added to the boiling water. This gave us the traditional 'Irish Stew'. Irish stew is mentioned in Molloy by the great Irish writer Samuel Beckett: ' Irish stew. A nourishing and economical dish, if a little indigestible. All honour to the land that has brought it before the world.'

$1^1/_2$ lb/675g lamb
$1^1/_2$ lb/675g potatoes
2 large onions
salt and pepper
1 teaspoon mixed herbs
$^3/_4$ pint/425 ml boiling water
1 meat-stock cube

Utensils: sharp knife, chopping board, potato peeler, oven-proof casserole dish, heat-proof measuring jug

---

Preheat the oven to gas mark 4 / 175 C° / 350 F°

---

1 Cut the lamb into cubes roughly 1 inch (2.5 cm) square, using a sharp knife on a chopping board – *! watch fingers.*

2 Peel the potatoes and cut them into slices about 1 inch thick (2.5 cm) – *! fingers.*

3 Peel the onions and chop then into thick slices – *! fingers.*

Onion tips: to prevent tears and stinging eyes, bite on a crust of dry bread while cutting the onions. It really works! To remove onion smells from your hands, wash them in milk.

4 Place layers of meat, onions, and potatoes in an oven-proof casserole dish, finishing with a layer of potatoes.

5 Season with salt and pepper and sprinkle the herbs on top.

6 Boil the water, dissolve the stock cube in it, and pour over the stew – *! watch the water.*

7 Cook for 2 hours and serve hot and steaming.

Apple Surprise

(serves 4)

Apples, which ripen in September and October, are Ireland's favourite fruit. They figure in the stories of Adam and Eve, William Tell (who shot an arrow through an apple placed on his son's head), and Sir Isaac Newton (who discovered the law of gravity after being hit on the head by a falling apple).

---

3 large cooking apples
1 small packet digestive biscuits
2oz/50g sugar
water

Utensils: mixing bowl, apple peeler, apple corer, sharp knife, oven-proof dish with lid, teaspoon

---

Preheat the oven to gas mark 5 / 190 C° / 375 F°

---

1 Place the biscuits in a mixing bowl and break into not-too-small pieces with your hands.

2 Peel the apples, remove the core, and cut into quarters. Cut into thin slices – *! watch fingers.*

3 Place a layer of biscuits in an oven-proof dish, then a layer of apple. Sprinkle with a teaspoon of water and a teaspoon of sugar.

4 Repeat the layers, finishing with a topping of crushed biscuits.

5 Bake with the lid on for 15-20 minutes, until the apples are soft.

6 Serve piping hot with cream or natural yogurt.

Moore Street Bananas

(serves 4)

In Dublin city, fruit and vegetables are sold in a famous open-air street market called Moore Street. Here the air is alive with the street-sellers' cries of 'apples and oranges, five for fifty' and 'bananas, luv, lovely bananas, luv'.

This yummy dessert is easy to make and just the thing for a cold winter's evening.

---

1 orange
4 Mars bars
4 large bananas
1oz/25g butter
1 tablespoon brown sugar

Utensils: orange squeezer, grater, sharp knife, chopping board, oven-proof dish, tablespoon

---

Preheat the oven to gas mark 7 / 425 F° / 220 C°

---

1 Squeeze the orange, using an orange squeezer (or by hand into a small bowl). Grate the orange rind carefully on the smallest grater blade – *! watch fingers.*

2 Cut the Mars bars into halves and the bananas into halves using a sharp knife – *! watch fingers.*

3 Place the bananas in an oven-proof dish and pour the orange juice over them. Spoon the orange rind over the banana slices.

4 Place a knob of butter on each banana slice and top with half a Mars bar.

5 Sprinkle each with brown sugar and bake for 10-15 minutes.

6 Eat while hot.

Gooey and gorgeous!

Banoffi

(serves 6-8)

Bananas are rich in vitamins and minerals and contain folate which is important for healthy blood cells. They can be used to make tasty bread and muffins but my very favourite way of serving them is on a cream, toffee and biscuit base. This is called Banoffi, a recipe from eastern Europe, which I first discovered when I went for tea at my friend Jo's house. Jo and her little sister had made a delicious Banoffi dessert and this is the recipe that I'm passing on to you.

12 digestive biscuits
4oz/100g butter
1 tin condensed milk (397g)
4 bananas
$^1/_2$ pint/275g cream
1 chocolate flake

Utensils: 2 saucepans, mixing bowl, wooden spoon, large cheesecake dish, chopping board, sharp knife, electric or hand-held whisk, metal spoon

1 Place the tin of condensed milk in a saucepan of boiling water – *! watch the water* – and simmer gently for 1 hour and 30 minutes. Make sure that there is plenty of water in the saucepan at all times.

2 While the milk is simmering, melt the butter in a saucepan over a low heat.

3 Crush the biscuits in a large mixing bowl with your hands or a wooden spoon.

4 Pour the melted butter over the biscuits and mix well – *! watch the hot butter.* Spoon the mixture into the cheesecake dish, covering the bottom evenly. Place in the fridge to set.

5 Just before you open the tin of milk, chop the bananas into chunky rounds. Whip the cream until peaks begin to form on the surface.

6 Remove the tin from the water and run it under cold water to cool it. Carefully open the tin. At this stage the milk will have turned into a rich toffee mixture – *! watch out for the hot toffee.*

7 Pour the toffee over the biscuit base and spread with a knife; if the toffee is too thick to pour, spoon it out. Cover the toffee with banana pieces.

8 Spoon the cream over the banana layer and sprinkle the chocolate flake over the top.

A heavenly, sweet treat for all the family!

Raspberry Cheesecake

(serves 6-8)

Raspberries thrive in Ireland because of the mild winters and the summer rain – one consolation for wet summer days! They have a wonderful flavour and taste great on this sweet biscuit base.

Raspberries are easy to grow (much easier than strawberries). We have raspberry bushes in our back garden and have fun picking and eating the ripe fruit in the summer. They also freeze well, so you can enjoy them all year round.

4oz/100g digestive biscuits
2oz/50g butter
8oz/225g cream cheese
1 punnet fresh raspberries or 8oz/225g tin
1 packet raspberry jelly
$^3/_4$ pint/425ml cream

Utensils: measuring jug, 2 mixing bowls, saucepan, wooden spoon, cheesecake dish, electric or hand-held whip

---

1 Melt the jelly in half a pint of boiling water in a heat-proof measuring jug. Leave to cool – *! watch the boiling water.*

2 Crush the biscuits in a large mixing bowl with your fingers or a wooden spoon.

3 Melt the butter in a saucepan and pour over the biscuits – *! watch the hot butter*. Mix together.

4 Spoon the biscuit mixture into the bottom of the cheesecake dish and leave aside.

5 Cream the cheese in a mixing bowl and add the raspberries. Put a few raspberries aside for later. Mix gently, trying not to crush the berries.

6 Add the jelly to the cream mixture.

7 Whip the cream and carefully fold into the cheese and jelly mix.

8 Pour the mixture on to the biscuit base and leave to set in the fridge for 3-4 hours.

9 Decorate the top with whole raspberries. Delicious!

Blackberry Crumble

(serves 4-6)

Crumble is easy, as long as you don't mind floury hands, and it makes a delicious, crunchy topping.

When my sisters and I returned to school every September, we liked to pick and eat blackberries on the walk home. Our mum would always know we had been feasting on them when she saw our stained hands and mouths.

Now my son Sam comes blackberry picking with me and we bring Coco, our dog. Then we bake blackberry crumble.

---

1 lb/450g blackberries
6oz/175g plain white flour
3oz/75g butter
6oz/175g sugar

Utensils: oven-proof bowl, mixing bowl, knife

Preheat the oven to gas mark 4 / 175 C° / 350 F°

---

1 Wash the blackberries carefully, removing any stalks or creepy crawlies! Place in the bottom of the ovenproof dish and sprinkle with half the sugar.

2 Place the flour in a mixing bowl. Cut the butter into small pieces and add to the flour – *! watch fingers.*

3 Rub the butter into the flour with your fingertips until the mixture looks like breadcrumbs. Add the rest of the sugar and mix together.

4 Sprinkle the crumble on to the blackberries and cook for 20-25 minutes.

5 Serve with cream or custard.

You can also make Apple Crumble in the same way. Use 4 peeled, cored and sliced cooking apples instead of the blackberries. Cooking takes slightly longer – 30-35 minutes.

Strawberry Ice-Cream

(serves 4-6)

We tend to think of ice-cream as a modern invention but in 1782 the Café Procope in Paris was serving over 72 different flavours. Home-made ice-cream is delicious and easy to make. This recipe uses tinned strawberries, so you can make it any time of the year. When fresh strawberries are in season (June and July), add them to the ice-cream to give it extra flavour.

1 tin strawberries
6oz/175g caster sugar
1 teaspoon lemon juice
$^1/_2$ pint/275ml cream
fresh strawberries (optional)

Utensils: electric blender, electric or hand-held whisk, 2 mixing bowls, metal spoon, shallow tin or metal dish

Set your freezer at the highest setting (ask an adult first)

1 Open the tin of strawberries and pour out about one third of the juice (freeze it as tasty ice-lollies). Place the remaining juice and the strawberries in an electric blender with the sugar and lemon juice. Swoosh together for 1-2 minutes until creamy – *! careful while using the blender.*

2 Pour the cream into a mixing bowl and whip until peaks begin to form on the surface.

3 Pour the strawberry mixture into the cream and blend together with a metal spoon. (Add a handful of fresh halved strawberries at this stage).

4 Pour the mixture into a shallow metal dish and place in the freezer until set (2-3 hours depending on the freezer).

5 Remove the ice-cream from the freezer 10-15 minutes before serving.

Criss-Cross Potatoes

(serves 4-6)

A family favourite in our house, these potatoes are very easy to make and taste great. Even the youngest member of our family, Sam (three), can help to cook these special potatoes.

---

4 large potatoes
2oz/50g butter

Utensils: sharp knife, baking tray

Preheat the oven to gas mark 6 / 400 F° / 200 C°

---

1 Scrub the potatoes and dry with kitchen roll or a clean tea-towel.

2 Cut each potato in half and place on a baking tray – *! watch fingers.*

3 Cut a criss-cross design (it should resemble a noughts and crosses game) into each potato and smear a knob of butter over the top.

4 Bake in the oven for 30 minutes until golden brown.

5 To make them extra special, sprinkle with grated cheddar cheese and bake for another 5-10 minutes until the cheese begins to bubble.

Potato Cakes

(makes 8)

In olden days most Irish people had a small plot of land on which they grew potatoes. In October they dug up the remainder of the potatoes that had not been eaten over the summer and stored them in a pile under a sheet of canvas or in a shed. Many different recipes were invented to use these left-over potatoes and this is one of them. The cakes were originally cooked on a griddle over the open fire. Potato cakes are known in Northern Ireland as fadge and in Cork as tatties or parleys.

---

6 potatoes
2oz/50g plain white flour
2oz/50g butter
1 egg
salt and pepper
knob of butter for frying

Utensils: potato peeler, saucepan, potato masher, knife, small bowl, fork, mixing bowl, wooden spoon, rolling pin, frying pan

---

1 Peel the potatoes, cut into thick slices – *! watch fingers* – and cook in boiling water until soft. Drain and mash – *! watch boiling water and steam.*

2 Melt the butter in a small saucepan. Beat the egg in a small bowl with a fork

3 Place all the ingredients in a mixing bowl, season with salt and pepper and mix together.

4 Sprinkle flour on to the table or counter-top and on to the rolling pin. Roll out the mixture into a rough circle a quarter of an inch thick. Cut into 8 triangles.

5 Place a knob of butter in the frying pan and fry each cake until golden brown, 8-10 minutes each side.

6 Serve hot with butter.

Potato cakes are delicious as part of a good old-fashioned Irish breakfast, served with bacon, eggs, sausages and tomatoes.

Donegal Boxty

(makes 8-10 cakes)

These little potato pats originated from Donegal, home of the spectacular Slieve League cliffs. They are the highest sea-cliffs in Europe and house hundreds of different sea birds.

In the North there is an old rhyme that warns:

Boxty on the griddle,
Boxty on the pan,
If you don't eat Boxty,
You'll never get your man!

8 medium potatoes
4oz/100g plain white flour
2oz/50g butter
salt and pepper
knob of butter for frying

Utensils: potato peeler, sharp knife, saucepan, potato masher, grater, mixing bowl, wooden spoon, rolling pin, circular cutter or cup, frying pan

1 First make the mashed potato. Peel the potatoes, cut into thick slices – *! watch fingers* – and cook in boiling water for 15-20 minutes. Drain and mash – *! watch the boiling water and steam.*

2 Peel the remaining potatoes and grate them – *! careful of fingers*. Dry the grated potato with kitchen roll or a clean tea-towel.

3 Cut the butter into small pieces – *! fingers*. Place all the ingredients in a mixing bowl and mix together. Add a pinch of salt and of pepper.

4 Place the mixture on a floured table top or counter-top and roll out with a floured rolling pin, to about a quarter of an inch thick. The flour prevents the mixture from sticking – so don't forget.

5 Using a circular cutter or a cup make 8-10 rounds.

6 Melt a little butter in the frying pan and cook each round until golden brown, 8-10 minutes each side.

7 Serve hot with extra butter.

Colcannon

(serves 4-6)

Colcannon was traditionally served at a harvest dinner, when the farmers and labourers needed a hot filling dinner after a day in the fields. It is also a Hallowe'en dish, when coins are wrapped in foil and hidden in the Colcannon, but watch those teeth!

There is an old Irish song which celebrates this great Irish dish:

Did you ever eat Colcannon
When 'twas made with yellow cream,
And the kale and praties blended
Like the picture in a dream?
Did you ever take a forkful,
And dip it in the lake
Of the heather-flavoured butter
That your mother used to make?

1 white cabbage
8 potatoes
4 onions
salt and pepper
1pint/570ml water
4oz/100g butter

Utensils: Sharp knife, chopping board, potato peeler, large saucepan, measuring jug, colander, potato masher, serving dish

1 Cut the cabbage into 4 pieces and remove the middle stump – *! watch fingers.*

2 Peel the potatoes and remove the outer layer of the onions – *! fingers.*

3 Chop the onions, cabbage and potatoes into slices half an inch thick – *! fingers.*

4 Place a layer of potatoes in the bottom of a large saucepan. Add a layer of onions, then a layer of cabbage. Season with a small pinch of salt and pepper.

5 Continue to add layers until all the vegetables are used up. Remember to season each layer.

6 Pour the water over the vegetables, bring to the boil and simmer for 25-30 minutes until all the vegetables are tender (test by slipping a skewer into the potatoes).

7 Drain the water using a colander – *! watch the steam, it can also burn.*

8 Mash the vegetables together, drop the butter into the middle and serve piping hot.

Champ

(serves 4-6)

It was a folk custom to leave a bowl of champ for the fairies at Hallowe'en. This was placed beside a fairy ring or under a hawthorn or blackthorn tree. Champ is usually made with potatoes and spring onions, but other ingredients can be used instead of spring onions at different times of the year, such as sorrell (a wild herb), nettles or fresh peas.

There was an old lady who lived in a lamp,
She had no room to beetle her champ.
So she up'ed with her beetle and broke her lamp,
And then she had room to beetle her champ.

(To beetle means to mash)

---

8 medium potatoes
6 spring onions
6oz/175g butter
$^{1}/_{4}$ pint/150 ml milk
salt and pepper

Utensils: potato peeler, sharp knife, chopping board, potato masher, saucepan, wooden spoon, measuring jug, serving dish

---

1 Peel the potatoes, cut into thick slices – *! watch fingers* – and cook in boiling water for 15-20

minutes. Drain and mash – *! watch the boiling water and steam.*

2 Remove the root ends, wash the spring onions and cut into small slices – *! watch fingers.*

3 Melt one third of the butter in a saucepan and add the milk and the spring onions. Bring to the boil and simmer for 2-3 minutes.

4 Add the potatoes and a pinch of salt and pepper and mix well. Cook for 5 minutes on a gentle heat, stirring occasionally.

5 Place in a serving dish and put the remaining butter in the middle to melt. Serve hot.

Hot New Potato Salad

(serves 4-6)

Irish new potatoes have a delicious flavour.

In the olden days, only the very rich could afford these 'early' potatoes, which are dug before they are fully grown. The people who depended on the potato for their staple diet had to plant main-crop potatoes, which gave much heavier yields, and these could not be dug until July. So when last year's crop was eaten, there was a hungry wait of some months until the new crop was ready.

---

1 lb/450g new potatoes
6 spring onions
4 heaped tablespoons mayonnaise
salt and pepper

Utensils: saucepan, skewer, sharp knife, chopping board, mixing bowl, tablespoon, serving dish

1 Wash the potatoes and cook in boiling water until they are soft enough to put a skewer through them.

2 Chop the spring onions finely – *! watch fingers.* Put aside some of the green top pieces.

3 Place the mayonnaise, spring onions and a large pinch of salt and pepper in a mixing bowl and stir together.

4 Drain the potatoes – *! watch the boiling water and steam* – and add them to the mayonnaise mix.

5 Serve hot. Sprinkle some of the green spring onion pieces over the top to give the dish colour.

Creamy Turnip

(serves 4-6)

The turnip, sometimes called the 'swede', was used in the olden days to feed cattle. During the famine it became an important vegetable and has been popular in Ireland ever since.

---

1 turnip
2oz/50g butter
salt and pepper

Utensils: peeler, sharp knife, saucepan, skewer, colander, masher, serving dish

---

1 Peel the turnip – *! watch fingers.*

2 Cut the turnip into quarters and then into cubes, using a sharp knife – *! fingers.*

3 Place the turnip in cold salted water, just enough to cover the pieces.

4 Bring the water to the boil and simmer for 20 minutes, until you can easily slip a skewer into the turnip pieces.

5 Drain carefully, using a colander – *! watch water and steam.* Mash the turnip, using a masher.

6 Cut the butter into pieces and add to the mashed turnip. Add a pinch of salt and pepper.

7 Place the turnip in a serving dish and eat hot.

Creamy and delicious!

Buttered Carrots

(serves 4-6)

While it was a World War II propaganda myth (put about to hide the invention of radar) that carrots enabled you to see in the dark, vitamin A is essential for vision in dim light.

---

8 medium carrots
2oz/50g butter
salt and pepper
2 teaspoons chopped parsley

Utensils: sharp knife, chopping board, saucepan, teaspoon

---

1 Wash and scrape the carrots with a sharp knife – *! watch fingers.*

2 Cut the carrots into rounds. Place them in a saucepan with just enough water to cover the pieces. Add a pinch of salt and half the butter.

3 Cook gently with the lid on for 12-15 minutes

until the carrots are tender (test with a skewer).

4 Remove the lid and continue cooking gently until all the water has been absorbed.

5 Add the rest of the butter and a pinch of salt and pepper.

6 Sprinkle with chopped parsley and serve steaming hot.

Cauliflower Cheese

(serves 4-6)

The cauliflower reached England during the sixteenth century from Spain and was then brought to Ireland. Cauliflowers grow well in Irish soil and are delicious topped with a creamy cheese sauce.

---

1 cauliflower
salt
1 packet cheese-sauce mix
$^1/_2$ pint/275ml milk (depending on mix)
1oz/25g grated white cheddar cheese

Utensils: sharp knife, chopping board, saucepan, small saucepan, wooden spoon, measuring jug, colander, serving dish

1 Remove the rough outer layers of the cauliflower. Cut away the stump and cut the cauliflower into quarters – *! watch fingers*. If you find this difficult, ask an adult to help.

2 Place the cauliflower in a saucepan, so that the rounded 'florets' are on the bottom of the pan. Add 1 inch of boiling water and a pinch of salt.

3 Cover the saucepan with a lid, bring to the boil and simmer for 12-15 minutes until tender.

4 While the cauliflower is cooking, make the sauce. You can make a home-made sauce if you like (ask an adult to help) but a mix is quicker and easier. Follow the instructions on the packet. Cooking time is usually about 5 minutes.

5 Drain the cauliflower using a colander – *! watch water and steam.*

6 Place the cauliflower in a dish, pour the sauce over the top and sprinkle with grated cheese.

Traditional Irish Salad

(serves 4)

Served with leftover cold meat as a lunch or supper dish, 'Irish' salad adds eggs, tomato, cucumber, beetroot, and mustard and cress to lettuce. Green vegetables and tomatoes are full of vitamins, especially C and E, which are important for growth and for healthy bodies. Mustard and cress is fun to grow, and shoots up very quickly. You can buy the seeds in a gardening shop and all they need is water.

---

1 butterhead lettuce
2 eggs
2 large tomatoes
half a cucumber
handful of mustard and cress
Dressing:
1 tablespoon white wine vinegar
3 tablespoons olive oil or vegetable oil
1 teaspoon mustard, seeded if possible
large pinch salt
large pinch pepper

Utensils: small saucepan, sharp knife, chopping board, screw-top container or small bowl and metal spoon, tablespoon, teaspoon

---

1 Put the eggs into a saucepan of water and boil gently for 10-12 minutes until hard. Crack the shells to prevent a black rim forming around the yoke and remove the shells when cool. Cut the eggs into quarters – *! watch those fingers*.

2 Wash the other salad ingredients.

3 Cut the tomatoes into quarters and the cucumber into slices – *! fingers again*. Separate the lettuce leaves.

4 Make the salad dressing by placing all the ingredients in a screw-top container and shaking together (or mix well in a small bowl).

5 Arrange the salad on 4 plates or in a large bowl. First a lettuce bed, then tomatoes, cucumber slices and egg pieces. Finally a sprinkle of mustard and cress over the top or 3 finely chopped spring onions.

6 Just before serving, pour the dressing over the salad.

Leprechaun Buns

(makes 14-16)

Leprechauns are the most industrious of the fairies, making shoes for all the Wee Folk. Said to be very rich, they hide their gold at the end of the rainbow. A poem by William Allingham describes how to make your fortune by catching one:

Lay your ear close to the hill.
Do you not catch the tiny clamour,
Busy click of an elfin hammer,
Voice of the leprechaun singing shrill
As he merrily plies his trade?
He's a span
And a quarter in height.
Get him in sight, hold him tight,
And you're a made man!

4oz/100g soft butter or margarine
4oz/100g caster sugar
2 eggs
4oz/100g self-raising flour
4-6oz/100-175g icing sugar
3-4 drops green food-colouring

Utensils: baking tray, large paper bun-cases, mixing bowl, wooden spoon, jug or small bowl, fork, metal spoon, wire cooling-rack, knife, teaspoon

Preheat the oven to gas mark 5 / 375 F° / 190 C°

1 Put the paper-cases on a baking tray and leave aside.

2 Put the butter and sugar in a mixing bowl and beat together with a wooden spoon until the mixture is light and creamy.

3 Beat the eggs in a jug or small bowl with a fork, and gradually add to the butter and sugar, mixing all the time with a wooden spoon.

4 Add the flour, bit by bit, and fold it in gently.

5 Spoon the mixture into the paper-cases and bake for 15-20 minutes until golden brown.

6 When cooked, cool the buns on a wire rack.

7 Mix the icing sugar with water, adding a little liquid at a time, until you form a smooth paste. Add a few drops of green food-colouring and mix in.

8 Spread the icing sugar on the buns with a teaspoon and allow to dry.

Fairy-Ring Cake

(makes 1 cake)

Irish fairies traditionally live in fairy forts or fairy rings. It is bad luck to build on such a ring as you will enrage the Wee Folk. Before building you should turn a sod on the site; if the fairies disapprove of the building they will turn it back at night.

Fairies were held responsible for much mischief in the olden days, such as turning milk or butter sour or replacing human babies with changelings or fairy babies.

6oz/175g soft butter
6oz/175g caster sugar
3 eggs
6oz/175g plain white flour
1½ teaspoons baking powder
¼ pint/150ml cream
2 tablespoons jam
6oz/175g icing sugar
2-3 tablespoons hot water
1 packet of Smarties or Jellytots

Utensils: 2 sandwich cake tins (8 inch), mixing bowl, wooden spoon, fork, small bowl, sieve, wire cooling-rack, hand-held whisk or electric mixer, knife or spatula

Preheat the oven to gas mark 4 / 350 F° / 175 C°

1 Grease the sandwich tins, using butter wrappers or butter on a piece of kitchen roll.

2 Place the butter and sugar in a large mixing bowl and beat with a wooden spoon until smooth and creamy.

3 Beat the eggs in a small bowl with a fork, and add to the sugar and butter mixture a little at a time. Stir the mixture until smooth.

4 Sift the flour and baking powder into the mixture and gently fold in. The mixture should be light and soft.

5 Pour half of the cake mixture into each of the tins and smooth down with a knife until the top is level.

6 Bake for 20-25 minutes until the cake halves are brown and risen.

7 Cool the halves on a wire rack.

8 Beat the cream in a small bowl, using a hand-held whisk or electric mixer. Spoon a layer of jam on to the bottom cake half. Add a layer of whipped cream. Sandwich the 2 halves together.

9 Mix the icing sugar with the water, adding a little of the liquid at a time until you can make a smooth paste. Spread the icing on the top of the cake, using a spatula or knife. Add the sweets in a circular pattern.

Chocolate Biscuit Cake

(makes 1 large cake)

When my sisters Kate and Emma and I were younger, there was a small shop down the road called Oswald's. We were allowed to walk to the shop on our own as it was on the same side of the road as our house. In this shop you could buy all kinds of goodies for a few pennies, including broken Kit-Kats and broken biscuits. They were kept in large glass jars behind the counter. Mum would transform these biscuits into a delicious chocolate-covered cake. The shop is no longer open, but we still enjoy Mum's broken-biscuit cake!

8oz/225g digestive biscuits
1oz/25g raisins, almonds, cherries or chocolate chips
4oz/100g milk chocolate
4oz/100g butter
2 tablespoons double cream

Utensils: shallow cake tin (8 inch), tin foil, mixing bowl, wooden spoon, saucepan

---

1 Line the tin with tin foil. Press gently around the

edges and be careful not to break the foil.

2 Put the biscuits in a large mixing bowl and break them into small pieces, using a wooden spoon or your fingers.

3 To the biscuits add raisins, almonds, cherries or chocolate chips (1 oz of each extra ingredient you choose).

4 Place the chocolate in a saucepan and heat gently. Add the butter and the cream and stir on a low heat until all the ingredients have melted together.

5 Pour the mixture on to the biscuits and stir gently. Make sure that all the biscuit pieces are covered with the chocolate mix.

6 Pour the mixture into the cake tin and cover with foil.

7 Leave in the fridge for about 2 hours to set.

Pooka Spice Biscuits

(makes 20-24 biscuits)

The pooka is an Irish spirit which haunts people every November. It takes the form or shape of an animal, usually a wild horse, that brings you on a terrifying ride on its back. These spicy biscuits are a perfect Hallowe'en snack and make a good 'trick or treat' gift. If you make a ghost or horse shape out of cardboard and use this as a pattern to cut around, your biscuits will be all the more appreciated.

10oz/275g plain white flour
1 level teaspoon baking powder
1 dessertspoon cinnamon
6oz/150g soft brown sugar
3oz/75g butter
1 egg
4 tablespoons golden syrup
currants for eyes

Utensils: large mixing bowl, teaspoon, dessertspoon, wooden spoon, knife, jug or small bowl, fork, tablespoon, rolling pin, baking tray, wire cooling-rack

Preheat the oven to gas mark 3 / 165 C°/ 325 F°

1 Place the flour, baking powder, cinnamon and sugar in a large mixing bowl and mix together.

2 Cut the butter into small pieces and add to the flour mixture. With your fingertips, rub the butter and the flour together until the mixture looks like breadcrumbs.

3 Break the egg into a jug and beat it with a fork. Add the golden syrup to the egg and stir. (To help the syrup slip off the spoon, heat the spoon in hot water first.)

4 Make a hollow in the flour mixture and gradually add the syrup and egg. Mix the ingredients together until you form a dough.

5 Sprinkle flour on to a table or counter-top and on to your rolling pin to prevent the mixture from sticking. Roll the dough out until it is about a quarter of an inch thick .

6 Make pooka shapes using a knife or make a simple, round shape using a cup.

7 Add currants for eyes and place on a floured baking tray.

8 Bake in the oven for 15-20 minutes until the biscuits are golden brown.

9 Place on a wire rack to cool.

Honey and Lemon Oatcakes

(makes 16-20)

In the olden days oats were grown and ground at home with a 'rotary quern'. These home-ground oats often contained pieces of stone or grit, which must have been hard on the teeth. In fact archaeologists have found Irish skeletons from medieval times with worn-down teeth!

Honey has been used as a flavouring and as a sweetener since early times. It was even used to flavour meat and fish dishes and was said to be great with salmon.

3oz/75g plain white flour
3oz/75g oatflakes
3oz/75g brown sugar
3oz/75g margarine
1 tablespoon honey
1 tablespoon lemon juice

Utensils: baking tray, mixing bowl, saucepan, tablespoon, wooden spoon, wire cooling-rack

---

Preheat the oven to gas mark 4 / 350 F° / 175 C

---

1 Grease the baking tray, using a butter wrapper or butter on a piece of kitchen roll.

2 Put the flour, oats and sugar into a mixing bowl.

3 Put the butter, honey and lemon juice into a saucepan and heat until the butter has melted. Tip: if you heat the spoon in hot water first, the honey will slide off without sticking.

4 Add the melted butter-mix to the dried ingredients and mix together well, using a wooden spoon.

5 Shape the dough into small balls with your hands (conker-size) and place them in the baking tray.

6 Bake for 15 minutes until golden brown.

7 Cool on the wire rack.

Pancakes

(makes 6-8 pancakes)

On Shrove Tuesday, or Pancake Day, pancakes were made to use up all the eggs and milk before the fasting of Lent. There is an old folk belief that if an unmarried girl can toss a pancake on Shrove Tuesday, she will be happily married within the year.

In our house, Pancake Day was looked forward to with great excitement. On arriving home from school, Mum would have a big pile of pancakes warm in the oven. We would spread butter on them, sprinkle them with sugar, roll them up and eat them with our fingers.

---

2 eggs
4oz/100g plain white flour
pinch of salt
$^1/_2$ a pint/275ml milk
lemon juice
caster sugar
knob of butter or oil for frying

Utensils: electric blender, mixing bowl, frying-pan

---

1 Place all the ingredients (except the caster sugar and lemon juice) into the blender and blend on high speed for 1 minute.

2 Pour into a bowl.

3 Heat the frying pan with a small knob of butter – *! watch out, the pan will be hot.* Pour about 2 table-spoons of batter into the pan, tilting the pan from side to side to cover the base with the mixture.

4 Cook for about 1 minute and then turn the pancake and cook for 30 seconds on the other side, until golden.

5 Continue cooking pancakes until all the batter is used up. If the pancakes begin to stick, add a little more butter. Keep the pancakes warm in the

oven on a low heat while you cook all the mixture.

6 Serve the pancakes with a squeeze of lemon and a sprinkle of castor sugar.

Real chefs toss the pancakes in the air to turn them – ask an adult to show you.

Mother's Day Cake

(makes 1 cake)

On Mother's Day or Mothering Sunday (the 4th Sunday in Lent) hard-working servant girls were given a day off to visit their families. They brought their mothers a rich simnel cake, a type of fruit cake with spices, to be eaten at Easter, after Lent. This recipe is for a lemon cake which will make a wonderful Mother's Day surprise.

1½ lemons
6oz/175g self-raising flour
6oz/175g caster sugar
4oz/100g soft margarine
2 eggs
3-4 tablespoons milk
2 tablespoons icing sugar

Utensils: grater, small plate, lemon squeezer, small bowl, mixing bowl, wooden spoon, baking tin (1 lb loaf tin), metal spoon

---

Preheat the oven to gas mark 4 / 350 F° / 175 C°

---

1 Cut one lemon in half, grate the rind on to a small plate, using the finest blade on the grater – *! watch fingers*. Squeeze both halves of the lemon into a small bowl.

2 Place the flour, sugar, margarine, eggs, milk, lemon rind and lemon juice into a large mixing bowl and mix together with a wooden spoon.

3 Spoon the mixture into the greased baking tin and cook for 1 hour. To test if it is ready, pierce the centre with a sharp knife; it should come out clean, with no sticky mixture on it. If there is, cook for another few minutes.

4 Squeeze the juice of the half lemon into a small bowl. Mix the icing sugar with the juice. Spoon the icing over the cake while it is still warm.

5 Put the cake on a wire rack to cool.

Shortbread

(makes 12-14 fingers)

When I was in the Brownies I cooked shortbread for a parents' day and it has been a favourite of mine ever since. The recipe uses cornflour, which is pure starch that has been separated from plain white flour.

9oz/250g plain white flour
3oz/75g cornflour
8oz/225g butter
3oz/75g caster sugar

Utensils: mixing bowl, sieve, saucepan, wooden spoon, shallow baking tin (15 by 20 cm), knife

Preheat the oven to gas mark 4 / 350 F° / 175 C°

1 Sieve the flour and cornflour into a mixing bowl. Add the sugar.

2 Melt the butter in a saucepan over a low heat – *! watch fingers* – and pour it slowly over the dry ingredients.

3 Mix well, using a wooden spoon.

4 Place the mixture in a greased, shallow baking tin.

5 Bake in the oven for 35-40 minutes.

6 When cooked, sprinkle some caster sugar over the top and cut into fingers.

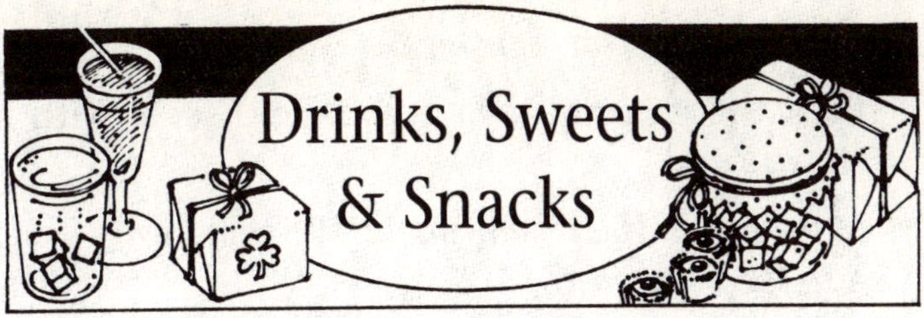

Drinks, Sweets & Snacks

St Patrick's Day Milk Shake

(makes 1 shake)

St Patrick, born around 385 AD, is the patron saint of Ireland. Every year we remember him on 17 March, St Patrick's Day, a festival not only in Ireland but all around the world wherever there are Irish communities. In some parts of America they even drink green beer!

Here's a beer-free 'green' drink for St Pat's Day.

---

1 banana
$^{1}/_{4}$ pint/150ml milk
2 tablespoons vanilla ice-cream
1 tablespoon honey
2-3 drops green food-colouring

Utensils: sharp knife, chopping board, electric blender, tablespoon, tall glass

---

1 Cut the banana into quarters.

2 Place all the ingredients in a blender and put the lid on (if you heat the spoon in hot water first, the honey will slide off). Blend for about 1

minute – *! be careful using the blender.*

3 Pour the mixture into a glass and serve with a straw. Yum!

Make a strawberry milkshake the same way, using 4oz/100g strawberries.

Old-Fashioned Lemonade

(serves 4-6)

In earlier times, before commercial fizzy drinks and fruit juices become available, people made their own drinks. These included nanadmin, a type of cider made from crab-apples; fraochan, made from wild blackberries; and mead, a wine made from honey.

This recipe for a refreshing lemon drink is quick and simple, perfect with ice on a hot summer's day. My son Sam loves making it and we use some of the mixture to make ice-lollies.

---

2 lemons
2 tablespoons white sugar
$1^1/_3$ pint/1 litre water

Utensils: sharp knife, chopping board, electric blender, sieve, large jug

---

1 Cut each of the lemons into 8 pieces, using a sharp knife on a chopping board – *! watch fingers.*

2 Place the lemon pieces in the blender with the sugar and water. Swoosh for 1-2 minutes.

3 Pour the juice into a large jug through a sieve.

4 Serve at once with lots of ice. This lemonade tastes best very fresh.

Top Hats

(makes 12-14)

Top Hats were always served at birthday parties when I was younger. I loved the look of the little chocolate and marshmallow treats, and I still enjoy making and eating them today.

---

1 packet cooking chocolate
1 packet marshmallows
1 packet Smarties or Jelly Tots
hundreds and thousands

Utensils: small bowl, metal spoon, teaspoon, small paper-cases

---

1 Place the chocolate in a small bowl and melt in the microwave. To melt on the cooker, place the bowl on a gently simmering saucepan of water and stir until the chocolate melts – *! careful of the boiling water.*

2 Place a teaspoon or more of chocolate into each paper-case, filling it half way up.

3 Place a marshmallow on the chocolate.

4 Put a little melted chocolate on each marsh-mallow and add a sweet. Sprinkle the top with hundreds and thousands.

Fudge

(makes 16-24 fudge pieces)

At Christmas, my friend Nikki always makes fudge to give to her friends and relations. She wraps it up in pretty boxes with ribbons. This fudge recipe always reminds me of her.

---

2 lb/900g soft brown sugar
$^{1}/_{2}$ lb/220ml butter
8 fluid oz/220 ml water
1 tin condensed milk (397g)

Utensils: saucepan, wooden spoon, measuring jug, teaspoon, saucer, shallow baking tray (15 by 20 cm), knife, spatula

---

1 Place the sugar, water and butter in a saucepan and boil for 5 minutes.

2 Add the condensed milk and stir until the mixture boils. Boil for 15 minutes, stirring with a wooden spoon.

3 Test the mixture to see if it's ready by dropping a teaspoon on to a saucer. If it sets at once then it's ready. If not, boil for a few more minutes.

4 When 'cooked', take the mixture off the heat and beat with a wooden spoon until it thickens.

5 Pour on to the baking tin and spread, using a spatula or knife.

6 When cool but not quite set, cut into squares, using a sharp knife.

Don't worry if your fudge is a little different each time you make it – that's fudge!

Shamrock Creams

(makes 16-24 creams)

The shamrock, worn on St Patrick's Day, is the traditional emblem of Ireland, like Scotland's thistle or the leek of Wales. A four-leafed shamrock is said to be lucky; it protects its owner from all 'pishogues' or spells.

---

1 teaspoon vegetable oil
1 egg
8oz/225g icing sugar
3 drops peppermint essence
3 drops green food-colouring

Utensils: greaseproof paper, large plate, mixing bowl, sieve, fork, small bowl, metal spoon, rolling-pin, sharp knife

1 Cover the plate with a piece of greaseproof paper. Pour a teaspoon of oil on to the paper and gently spread with your fingers (this will prevent the sweets from sticking to the paper as they dry).

2 Separate the egg and put the white into a mixing bowl.

3 Sieve the sugar into a bowl.

4 Beat the egg white gently. Be careful not to beat until stiff.

5 Add the sugar to the egg white, a little at a time, and beat until smooth.

6 Add 3 drops of peppermint essence and 3 drops of food colouring to the mixture and mix in well. Put the drops on to a teaspoon before adding, as this will stop you adding too much.

7 Sprinkle a little icing sugar on the table or counter-top. Rub some also on the rolling-pin to ensure the mixture doesn't stick.

8 Knead the mixture gently, roll out to a $^1/_2$ inch thickness and cut into shamrock shapes or little rounds, using a sharp knife – *! watch fingers.*

9 Leave to dry on the papered plate overnight and store in an airtight container when hard.

Tricolour Fruit Kebabs

(makes 5-6 kebabs)

Fruit is sweet, low in fat and full of vitamins and minerals, such as vitamins A, B and C. Vitamin C is important for the absorption of iron and the growth of body tissue, and can also aid recovery from illness. Fruit is also a good source of fibre which helps digestion and heart function. As the old saying goes, 'An apple a day keeps the doctor away'.

Exotic fruits, such as kiwis and melons, are now readily available.

---

2 apples
2 oranges
1 melon
2 kiwi fruit
2 peaches
bunch of green grapes
juice of half a lemon

Utensils: apple peeler, sharp knife, chopping board, wooden kebab sticks

---

1 Peel the apples, using a peeler. Cut into quarters and remove the cores using a sharp knife – *! watch fingers*. Dip the pieces in lemon juice to prevent them turning brown. Cut into bite-sized pieces.

2 Peel the oranges and separate into segments. Cut each segment in half.

3 Cut the melon in half and remove the pips. Put one half aside. Cut the other into eighths and then into bite-sized cubes.

4 Peel the kiwi fruit, using the peeler, and cut into quarters.

5 Wash the peaches, cut each in half, remove the stones and cut into bite-sized chunks.

6 Wash the grapes, cut each in half and remove the pips.

7 Put the fruit on the kebab sticks – *! watch fingers as they can be sharp.* Assemble in a green, white and orange pattern. For example – grape, apple, orange; kiwi fruit, apple, peach. Continue until all the fruit is used up.

8 Display the sticks in the melon half.

For a cool summer snack, place the sticks in the fridge for an hour before serving.

BLT (Bacon – Lettuce – Tomato) Specials

(makes 2 BLTS)

My friend Paul, who I used to sail with, first introduced me to BLTs. These hot sandwiches were just the thing to fill us up after a hard day's sailing.

Use Irish bacon (maple cured is my favourite) and Irish red cheddar for the best results.

---

1 packet Irish bacon (8 slices)
2 tomatoes
1 onion
handful of lettuce
4oz/100g cheddar cheese
6 slices bread
2 tablespoons mayonnaise
black pepper

Utensils: sharp knife, chopping board, grater, toaster

---

1 Place the bacon under the grill and cook on medium heat for 5-6 minutes on each side, until brown and crispy

2 While the bacon is cooking, slice the tomatoes, using a sharp knife. Chop the onion into small pieces and shred the lettuce – *! watch fingers*.

3 Grate the cheese. Toast the bread lightly in the toaster.

4 When the bacon and toast are ready, begin to build the BLTs as follows:

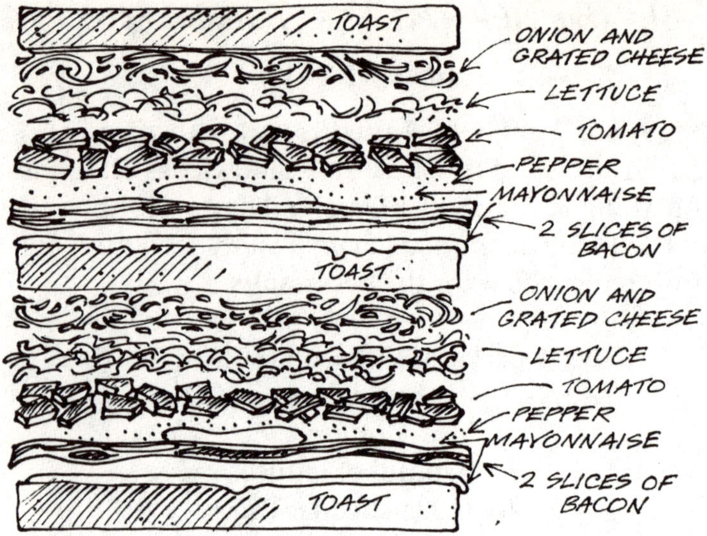

a slice of toast spread with some mayonnaise
2 slices of bacon
a dollop of mayonnaise
a pinch of pepper
sliced tomato and lettuce
a sprinkle of onions and grated cheese
a slice of toast spread with mayonnaise
repeat the bacon, mayonnaise, tomato,
onion and grated cheese
top with a slice of toast
(Don't worry if some of the ingredients fall
on to the plate!)

5 Cut each BLT in half and serve hot or cold.

A messy hunger-quenching snack!

Bread

Irish Brown Bread

(makes 3 x 1 lb loaves)

Ireland is famous for its brown bread. In olden days it was baked on an open fire in a pot-oven. This 'oven' was a heavy black pot with a lid, which was placed on the open fire and covered with hot coals or burning turf. The bread was removed when cooked and placed on the window-sill to cool. This recipe uses many different flours, all of which are full of goodness.

11/2 lb/675g brown flour
8oz/225g plain white flour
4oz/100g oatmeal
4 teaspoons breadsoda
3 teaspoons sugar
3 teaspoons salt
1¾ pint/1000ml buttermilk

Utensils: large mixing bowl, wooden spoon, measuring jug, 3 x 1 lb loaf tins, wire cooling-rack

---

Preheat the oven to gas mark 7 / 425 F° / 220 C°

---

1 Place all the dry ingredients in a large mixing bowl and add the buttermilk, a little at a time.

2 Mix together well, using a wooden spoon. Unlike other dough, the mixture will be wet and sloppy.

3 Pour the mixture into the loaf tins and bake for 40-45 minutes.

4 Place on a wire rack to cool.

Griddle Bread

(serves 4-6)

Griddle bread got its name from the hot-plate or 'griddle' on which it was cooked. The griddle was a round iron plate which had two handles or 'ears'. It rested on a small three-legged stand over the open fire.

Now cooked in a frying-pan, griddle bread is wonderful served hot with melted butter.

8oz/225g plain flour
1 teaspoon baking powder
pinch of salt
1oz/25g sugar
1oz/25g butter
$^{1}/_{4}$ pint/150ml milk
1 egg
knob of butter for frying

Utensils: mixing bowl, sieve, small bowl, fork, saucepan, wooden spoon, knife

---

1 Sieve the flour, salt and baking powder into a large mixing bowl and add the sugar.

2 Beat the egg in a small bowl using a fork. Melt the butter in a saucepan. Add the melted butter, milk and egg to the other ingredients and mix together well with a wooden spoon. The mixture will be creamy.

3 Place a large knob of butter in a frying-pan and melt over a moderate heat.

4 Place the mixture in the pan and cook for 8-10 minutes on each side.

5 When cooked, divide the bread into 6-8 triangular pieces and serve hot with butter.

White Soda Bread

(makes 1 loaf)

When I was small my Mum sometimes made a loaf of white soda bread, which we all helped to stir and knead. The smell of bread baking was mouth-watering and I loved eating it warm, with melting butter.

Soda bread is easy to make and makes a delicious change to the normal yeast-based pans.

---

1 lb/450g plain white flour
1 teaspoon baking powder
1 level teaspoon salt
1 teaspoon sugar
1/2 pint/275ml buttermilk

Utensils: mixing bowl, sieve, wooden spoon, knife, baking tray, wire cooling-rack

---

Preheat the oven to gas mark 6 / 400 F° / 200 C°

---

1 Sieve the flour and baking powder into a mixing bowl. Add the sugar and salt.

2 Make a well (small hole) in the middle of the flour and pour in the milk.

3 Mix together with a wooden spoon to form a dough.

4 Knead on a lightly floured table or counter-top for 3-4 minutes.

5 Shape the dough into a circle and cut a criss-cross in the top to prevent it from cracking when baking. Place on a floured baking tray and bake for 40-45 minutes.

6 Place on a wire rack to cool.

Scones

(makes 12-14 scones)

Ireland has a great tradition of baking cakes and special breads. Skills were passed down from mother to daughter and the most prized compliment was that you had 'a light hand with the baking'.

Scones are delicious served with cream and jam. Even more delicious in summer with fresh strawberries and cream.

8oz/225g self raising flour
a pinch of salt
1 1/2 oz/38g butter
1oz/25g sugar
2oz/50g currants (optional)
1/4 pint/150ml milk

Utensils: mixing bowl, wooden spoon, rolling pin, round pastry cutter or cup, baking tray, wire cooling-rack

Preheat oven to gas mark 7 / 425 F° / 220 C°

1 Place the flour in a mixing bowl and add a pinch of salt.

2 Rub the butter into the flour with your finger-tips, until the mixture looks like breadcrumbs.

3 Stir in the sugar and currants.

4 Add the milk and mix with a wooden spoon. Using your hands, draw the dough together and place on a floured table-top or counter.

5 Using a floured rolling pin, roll the dough out until it is about 1 inch thick. Cut rounds with a pastry cutter or cup.

6 Dust the scones with a little flour, place on a greased baking tray and bake for 12-15 minutes.

7 Place the scones on a wire cooling-rack to cool, or serve warm with butter or cream and jam.

Hot Herb Bread

(serves 6-8)

It is a family favourite, and when I was very small my Mum would let me butter the herb stick and press it together. Ideal as a starter or with a main meal, hot herb bread is bound to be a hit!

Try using different breads such as Vienna roll or brown bread as well as French stick.

---

1 French stick
4oz/100g butter
pinch salt
$^1/_2$ teaspoon pepper
1 tablespoon mixed herbs
1 teaspoon lemon juice
2 cloves crushed garlic (optional)

Utensils: bread knife, bread board or chopping board, mixing bowl, metal spoon, knife, tin foil, baking tray

---

Preheat the oven to gas mark 6 / 200 C° / 400 F°

---

1 Cut the bread into slices 1 inch thick, but be careful not to cut through to the bottom crust – *! watch fingers.*

2 Place the butter, herbs, salt, pepper, lemon juice and crushed garlic in a mixing bowl and cream together, using a metal or wooden spoon. You can warm the butter first to make it easier.

3 Butter each piece of bread with the mixture, on each side, and press together to reform the stick.

4 Wrap in tin foil and place on a baking tray.

5 Cook for 15-20 minutes and serve hot.

Barm Brac

(makes 1 loaf)

In the nineteenth century, brac was associated with New Year's Eve. If you threw a piece of brac against the back of your front door you would be rich all year. These days it is associated with Hallowe'en and special things are wrapped up and added to the brac to tell your fortune. A wedding-ring means you will be married within the year, a coin means wealth, a pea means poverty and a thimble means you will never be married.

Brac means speckled and barm (not 'barn' as some people say) is the old word for a liquid which raised the loaf.

4oz/100g soft brown sugar
8oz/200g mixed fruit
1 cup tea
1 egg
8oz/200g self-raising flour

Utensils: mixing bowl, cup, wooden spoon, 1 x 1 lb loaf tin

Preheat the oven to gas mark 4 / 350 F° / 175 C°

---

1 Place the fruit and sugar in a large mixing bowl and soak in 1 cup of tea for 1 hour (or longer if possible).

2 Stir in the egg and the flour gently with a wooden spoon.

3 Place the mixture in a greased loaf tin and bake for 1 hour.

4 Serve warm or cold with butter.

Tom McCaughren's Scotch Eggs

(serves 4)

'In my wildlife books you will find that foxes are very fond of eggs. They in turn find that other animals also have a great liking for them. In *Run Swift, Run Free,* for example, the young foxes discover that a stoat will steal an egg from a nest and trundle it along the ground with its nose until it reaches a secluded place where it can savour the contents in peace. They also discover, to their cost, that if they steal the egg from the stoat, the stoat won't be a bit pleased.

In the same chapter of *Run Swift, Run Free,* Old Sage Brush is showing the young foxes the ways of the wild. They find a pheasant's nest. All the shells are broken and empty and they wonder what has happened to them.

Being the wise old fox that he is, Old Sage Brush goes on to explain that they will know what has been at the nest by the way the shells have been broken. "The grey crow or magpie", he tells them, "will peck a hole in the egg, then put in the upper part of its beak, lift it up and drink it. The hedgehog will bite a large hole in the egg and lick out the yolk with its tongue. The stoat will bite a small hole in the end of it and get at the yolk that way.'

So the question is, what happened to the pheasant's eggs? They'd been broken in half and some of them were tucked inside each other. As it turns out, they hadn't been eaten at all. So what do you think happened to them? While you're trying to figure that out, here's a recipe for an egg that would be an even greater puzzle for the foxes – it's for a Scotch egg.'

---

4 hard boiled eggs
1oz/25g plain white flour
2258oz/g pork sausage meat
breadcrumbs
1 beaten egg

Utensils: mixing bowl, knife, bread board, deep fat frier

Preheat the frier to 340° F / 170° C

---

1 Toss eggs in flour. Split sausage meat into 4 pieces and, on a floured bread board, roll each piece into a circle that will fit around the egg (don't forget to flour the board or the meat will stick to it).

2 Cover the eggs in the sausage meat. Roll each egg in beaten egg mixed with breadcrumbs. Deep fry for 8 minutes – *! watch the hot oil.*

3 Drain off the excess oil in kitchen paper and serve hot or cold.

Marita Conlon-McKenna's Gluten-Free Brownies

(makes 12-14 brownies)

'Being on a gluten-free diet is a bit of a pain! Ever since I was a teenager, I have been allergic to flour as I have Coeliac Disease. One of my children, Fiona is unable to eat flour too – so at home we have developed a recipe for the best gluten-free Brownies in the world. Unfortunately because they taste so good the whole family eats them and they are gone in a flash.'

4oz/100g butter
4oz/100g plain chocolate
4oz/100g soft brown sugar
4oz/100g gluten-free flour
pinch of salt
2 beaten eggs
1-2 tablespoons milk
icing sugar to sift

Utensils: 20cm / 8 inch square cake tin, small mixing bowl, wooden spoon, saucepan, sieve, tablespoon, wire cooling rack

---

Preheat the oven to gas mark 4 / 175 C° / 350 F°

---

1 Grease the cake tin with a butter wrapper.

2 Place the butter and chocolate in a bowl set over

a saucepan of hot water. Stir with a wooden spoon until the chocolate and butter melt.

3 Remove the bowl from the heat, stir in the sugar and leave to cool.

4 Sift the flour and salt into a mixing bowl. Make a well in the centre and pour in the chocolate mixture.

5 Add the eggs and beat well with a wooden spoon.

6 Add enough milk to make a moist mixture which will pour.

7 Pour the mixture into the cake tin and bake for 30 minutes.

8 Leave to cool on a wire rack, then cut into squares and sift a little icing sugar over the top of each brownie.

Aishlinn O'Loughlin's Appley Ever After Cake

(serves 6-8)

'Poor old Snow White hadn't much luck when it came to apples, did she? Or maybe she did. After all, of it hadn't been for eating that apple, she would never have met her Prince Charming. Still, I can think of better ways of meeting your husband than by choking on an apple, and I can think of better things to do with apples than choking on them.'

Here's one thing (to do with apples that is, not

one way to meet your husband – although you never know ...).

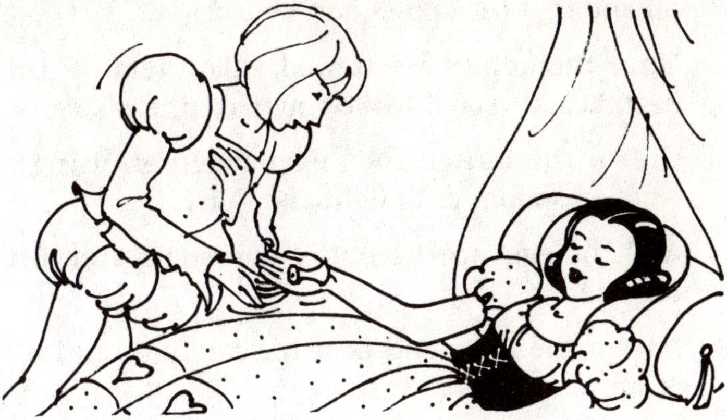

2 large cooking apples
2 dessertspoons sugar
6oz /175g castor sugar
6oz /175 g butter
8oz /225g self-raising flour
3 large eggs (beaten)

Utensils: apple corer, sharp knife, chopping board, saucepan, mixing bowl, wooden spoon, large baking tin

Preheat the oven to gas mark 6 / 400 F° / 200 C°

1 Wash and chop the cooking apples into thick slices – you don't have to peel them if you don't want to. Put them in a saucepan, add the sugar and enough water to just cover them.

2 Cook at a high temperature for about 10 minutes. Make sure that the water doesn't boil off and that the apples don't burn.

3 Once the apples are stewed, take them off the heat. Leave to cool while you make the cake mix.

4 Cream the butter and sugar together, using a wooden spoon, until light and fluffy.

5 Add the eggs to the butter and sugar and mix together.

6 Mix in the flour and beat the mixture until it's creamy.

7 Grease the baking tin and pour in half the cake mix.

8 Spread the stewed apple on top and cover with the rest of the cake mix.

9 Bake for 1 hour, until the top is golden and crispy.

Gorgeous, either on its own or covered with whipped cream. But if you're going to top it with cream, leave it to cool for a while or the cream will melt.

Gorden Snell's Mackerel Smokies

(serves 6)

Gorden Snell is a popular children's author, whose books include *The Tex and Sheelagh Omnibus* and *The Mystery of Monk Island*. Gordon has also written *The Rhyming Irish Cookbook*.

1 lb/450g smoked mackerel
½ pint /275ml cream
12 small mushrooms
2oz/50g grated Parmesan cheese
pepper
butter

Utensils: fork, 6 small pots or ramekins, sharp knife, chopping board

Preheat the oven to gas mark 5 / 375 F° / 190 C°

1 Break the mackerel into flakes using a fork.

2 Take six small pots or ramekins and smear butter round the insides.

3 Nearly fill each pot with the mackerel.

4 Slice the mushrooms thinly and add some to each pot.

5 Pour cream into each pot, then sprinkle on Parmesan cheese and a little pepper.

6 Put the pots in the oven and bake for 20 minutes.

Splendid as tea-time snacks or perfect party starters.

Raymondo's Spaghetti

(serves 2)

This is Ray D'arcy's (Den TV) favourite spaghetti dish. Dustin the turkey loves it but he doesn't know what's in it. If he knew about the anchovies he might not eat it!

Try it and see if you can taste the anchovies.

---

2 anchovies
2 cloves garlic
olive oil
1 tin chopped tomatoes
1oz /25g olives, capers, basil
250g/ 9oz spaghetti

Utensils: frying pan, sharp knife, chopping board, saucepan, wooden spoon

---

1 Chop up the anchovies and garlic and put in a frying-pan with some olive oil.

2 Cook the mixture until soft – it will be brown and 'gooey'.

3 Add the tin of chopped tomatoes.

4 Add the olives, capers and basil.

5 Cook for 7 minutes.

6 Meanwhile, cook the spaghetti in boiling water (12-15 minutes).

7 Mix the cooked pasta with the sauce and serve.

Vera Pettigrew's
Tasty Treats for Camp Fires

(serves any number)

'Have you ever sat around a camp fire to sing songs with your friends on a summer's evening, or stood beside a Hallowe'en bonfire on a winter's night as the sparks fly upwards into the starry sky? If you have, you will know that it's hungry work, so why not cook something hot and tasty?'

---

1 banana for each person
1 small chocolate bar for each person

Utensils: knife, tin foil, tongs or long-handled fork

---

1 Slit open the bananas length-wise but not quite to the ends.

2 Place the chocolate bars inside and close up.

3 Wrap each banana in tin foil and put in the glowing embers of the fire.

4 Cook for 5 to 10 minutes.

5 Remove from the fire with a tongs or long-handled fork – *! be careful not to get burned.*

Vera Pettigrew has organized many scout and girl guide camps. She is the author of *Fionuala the Glendalough Goat* and *The Adventures of Henry & Sam & Mr Fielding.*

Marita Conlon-McKenna's Honey-Men Biscuits

(makes 8-12 men)

'All my children loved to hear the story of The Gingerbread Man. However none of them liked the taste of ginger and wouldn't eat shop bought 'gingerbread men'. So we invented our own men and we call them 'honey men'. They look just as good but taste nicer!'

4oz/100g sugar
4oz/100g butter
8oz/225g flour
1 tablespoon milk
1 tablespoon honey
currants for decoration

Utensils: mixing bowl, wooden spoon, sieve, rolling-pin, gingerbread man shape cutter or sharp knife, baking tray, wire cooling-rack

---

Preheat oven to gas mark 4 / 350 F° / 175 C°

---

1 Mix butter, sugar and honey together in a mixing bowl, using a wooden spoon.

2 Sift in the flour and then add in the milk.

3 Mix together and roll out the dough on a floured surface, using a floured rolling-pin.

4 Cut the dough into 'man' shapes with a cutter or a sharp knife.

5 Decorate each man with currants for eyes.

6 Bake for 12 – 15 minutes.

7 Cool on a wire rack before eating.

Aislinn O'Loughlin's Rummy's Yummy Lemon Parcels

(serves 3)

'If you've read *A Right Royal Pain* by yours truly, you'll know that Rumpelstiltskin didn't deserve the bad reputation he's been dumped with (and if you haven't read it, Why Not?). But I bet you didn't know that Rummy also loved cooking. It's true! Especially sweet things. Here's one of his favourite recipes – updated a bit, of course.'

---

6 slices white bread (without the crusts)
lemon curd
oil for frying
1 beaten egg
whipped cream

Utensils: knife, frying pan

---

1 Spread a generous amount of lemon curd on one slice of bread and put another slice on top. Repeat three times, so that you have 3 lemon curd sandwiches.

2 Heat some oil in the pan. Dip the sandwiches in the egg, and fry until golden brown on both sides.

3 Leave to cool before topping with cream (it's a healthy idea to drain off as much oil as you can by wrapping the parcels in kitchen paper when you take them out of the frying-pan).

4 And there you have it! Rummy's treat, ready for you to enjoy. But don't try to eat them all yourself, only certified O'Loughlin pigs can manage that without ending up with a sore tummy.

Cheat's tip: Try making the parcels in a toasted sandwich-maker by buttering both sides of the sandwich and toasting for a few minutes. But don't dip these ones in egg first or you'll end up with a very big mess – and I'll get the blame.

Maeve Morris's
Eggscape with Ham and Cheese

(serves 1 – me)

'Can't say I like cooking. All that chopping and dicing and shredding and mixing and kneading and slaving over a hot stove. The result is usually overcooked or undercooked, sunken or inedible.

The one recipe you can't go wrong with is my Eggscape – even Jamie who's been to Paris thinks it's brill.'

---

1 slice of wholemeal bread
1 egg
oil for cooking
butter
1 slice ham
a good sprinkling of grated cheese
black pepper
a sprig of parsley

Utensils: toaster, frying-pan, grater

---

1 Lightly toast the bread.

2 Fry the egg in a little vegetable oil.

3 Butter the toast and put the slice of ham on top.

4 Put the fried egg on top of the ham and sprinkle with the cheese.

5 Place under the grill until the cheese melts.

6 Sprinkle with black pepper and serve with a sprig of parsley.

I sprang to the grill-pan
And, oh, golly gee!
I sizzled, pan sizzled,
Egg sizzled – all three.
If you value your fingers
Or even your hair,
Look out for hot grill pans
And take lots of care.

The three Maeve Morris adventures by Mary Arrigan are: *Dead Monks and Shady Deals*, *Landscape with Cracked Sheep* and *Seascape with Barber's Harp*.

After you finish

1) Make sure the cooker is switched off and any electrical machines are off and unplugged.
2) Put away any leftover ingredients. Milk, eggs, cheese and meat must be put back in the fridge, along with any other food that might go off.
3) Wash and dry all the dirty utensils and put them away. This is the un-fun bit! But you could get a friend or parent to help, maybe even a little sis.
4) Clean down the worktops and tabletops.
5) Leave everything clean and tidy.

Index

For easy reference, the sections of the book are printed in capital letters, the recipes in italics.

Author

SARAH WEBB is the children's book buyer at Waterstone's in Dawson Street, Dublin. She lives in Dalkey, eight miles south of Dublin city, in a converted coach house, with her son Sam. Sarah is a founding member of Children's Books Ireland and organises children's book events for adults and children.

In her spare time she likes reading, cooking (and eating!) and sailing. Her favourite food is ice-cream. Her favourite books? Diplomatically she says she reads practically everything, loves five per cent and likes another eighty-five per cent.

Kids Can Cook is her first published book; she also writes short stories, poetry, and articles for newspapers and magazines.

My Own Recipes

My Own Recipes